AF293163

Defoe
Abbott
Marx
Hardy
Melville
Machiavelli
Montaigne
Carroll
Christie
Chesterton
Cooper
Emerson
Joyce
Austen
Hugo
Eliot
Grimm
Stoker
Wilde
Haggard
Molière
Maupassant
Byron
Schiller
Engels
Smith
Kafka
Hall
Garnett
Goethe
Cotton
Einstein
Fitzgerald
Hawthorne
Dostoyevsky
Baum
Henry
Kipling
Doyle
Willis
Leslie
Dumas
Flaubert
Turgenev
Nietzsche
Balzac
Stockton
Vatsyayana
Crane
Burroughs
Verne
Curtis
Tocqueville
Whitman
Gogol
Vinci
Homer
Widger
Tolstoy
Busch
Darwin
Thoreau
Twain
Scott
Plato
Potter
Freud
Zola
Lawrence
Dickens
Harte
Kant
Jowett
Stevenson
Burton
Hesse
Andersen
London
Descartes
Cervantes
Voltaire
Poe
Aristotle
Wells
Cooke
Hale
James
Hastings
Bunner
Shakespeare
Irving
Richter
Chambers
da
Chekhov
Shaw
Doré
Dante
Swift
Benedict
Wodehouse
Pushkin
Alcott
Newton

Fires of Driftwood

Isabel Ecclestone Mackay

Imprint

This book is part of TREDITION CLASSICS

Author: Isabel Ecclestone Mackay
Cover design: Buchgut, Berlin – Germany

Publisher: tredition GmbH, Hamburg - Germany
ISBN: 978-3-8424-4865-0

www.tredition.com
www.tredition.de

Copyright:
The content of this book is sourced from the public domain.

The intention of the TREDITION CLASSICS series is to make world literature in the public domain available in printed format. Literary enthusiasts and organizations, such as Project Gutenberg, worldwide have scanned and digitally edited the original texts. tredition has subsequently formatted and redesigned the content into a modern reading layout. Therefore, we cannot guarantee the exact reproduction of the original format of a particular historic edition. Please also note that no modifications have been made to the spelling, therefore it may differ from the orthography used today.

FIRES OF DRIFTWOOD

BY ISABEL ECCLESTONE MACKAY

WITH DECORATIONS BY J.E.H. MACDONALD A.R.C.A.

First published by McClelland & Stewart, Limited, Toronto, 1922.

The thanks of the author are due to the editors of *Ainslee's Magazine, The American Magazine, The Canadian Magazine, Canadian Home Journal, The Canadian Bookman, The Forum, The Globe, Harper's Magazine, The Independent, The Ladies' World, McClure's Magazine, Metropolitan Magazine, The Reader Magazine, Scribner's Magazine, Saturday Night,* and *The Youth's Companion* for permission to publish this verse in its present form.

CONTENTS

- THE HAPPY TRAVELLER
- THE DEAD BRIDE
- THE CROCUS BED
- THE VISION
- THE MIRACLE
- THE HOMESTEADER
- WET WEATHER
- THE SLEEPING BEAUTY
- DOWN AT THE DOCKS
- LAKE LOUISE
- THE GATEKEEPER
- THE BRIDGE BUILDER
- THE PRAIRIE SCHOOL
- CALGARY STATION
- VALE
- THE WAY TO WAIT
- THE PASSER BY
- FIRST LOVE
- SAD ONE, MUST YOU WEEP
- JOSEPH
- A CHRISTMAS CHILD
- SPRING IN NAZARETH
- INHERITANCE
- SONG OF THE SLEEPER
- THE TYRANT
- THE GIFTS
- THE TOWN BETWEEN
- ON THE MOUNTAIN
- THE PROPHET
- GIVE ME A DAY
- LITTLE BROWN BIRD
- THE WATCHER
- POSSESSION
- TO ARCADY
- THE FIELDS OF EVEN
- I LOVE MY LOVE

Fires of Driftwood

*ON what long tides
Do you drift to my fire,
You waifs of strange waters?
From what far seas,
What murmurous sands,
What desolate beaches —
Flotsam of those glories that were ships!*

*I gather you,
Bitter with salt,
Sun-bleached, rock-scarred, moon-harried,
Fuel for my fire.*

*You are Pride's end.
Through all to-morrows you are yesterday.
You are waste,
You are ruin,
For where is that which once you were?*

*I gather you.
See! I set free the fire within you —
You awake in thin flame!
Tremulous, mistlike, your soul aspires,
Blue, beautiful,
Up and up to the clouds which are its kindred!
What is left is nothing —
Ashes blown along the shore!*

When as a Lad

WHEN, as a lad, at break of day
I watched the fishers sail away,
My thoughts, like flocking birds, would follow
Across the curving sky's blue hollow,
And on and on—
Into the very heart of dawn!

For long I searched the world—ah, me!
I searched the sky, I searched the sea,
With much of useless grief and rueing
Those wingid thoughts of mine pursuing—
So dear were they,
So lovely and so far away!

I seek them still and always must
Until my laggard heart is dust
And I am free to follow, follow,
Across the curving sky's blue hollow,
Those thoughts too fleet
For any save the soul's swift feet!

Laureate

DEATH met a little child who cried
For a bright star which earth denied,
And Death, so sympathetic, kissed it,
Saying: "With me
All bright things be!"—
And only the child's mother missed it.

Death met a maiden on the brae,
Her eyes held dreams life would betray,
And gallant Death was greatly taken—
"Leave," whispered he,
"Your dream with me
And I will see you never waken."

Death met an old man in a lane;
So gnarled was he and full of pain

That kindly Death was struck with pity —
"Come you with me,
Old man," said he,
"I'll set you down in a fair city."

So, kingly Death along the way
Scatters rare gifts and asks no pay —
Yet who to Death will write a sonnet?
If any dare,
Let him take care
No foolish tear be spilled upon it!

Out of Babylon

THEIR looks for me are bitter,
And bitter is their word —
I may not glance behind unseen,
I may not sigh unheard.

So fare we forth from Babylon,
Along the road of stone;
And no one looks to Babylon
Save I — save I alone!

My mother's eyes are glory-filled
(Save when they fall on me)
The shining of my father's face
I tremble when I see,

For they were slaves in Babylon,
And now they're walking free —
They leave their chains in Babylon,
I bear my chains with me!

At night a sound of singing
The vast encampment fills;
"Jerusalem! Jerusalem!"
It sweeps the nearing hills —

But no one sings of Babylon
(Their home of yesterday)

And no one prays for Babylon,
And I—I dare not pray!

Last night the Prophet saw me;
And, while he held me there,
The holy fire within his eyes
Burned all my secret bare.

"What! Sigh you so for Babylon?"
(I turned away my face)
"Here's one who turns to Babylon,
Heart traitor to her race!"

I follow and I follow!
My heart upon the rack;
I follow to Jerusalem—
The long road stretches back

To Babylon, to Babylon!
And every step I take
Bears farther off from Babylon
A heart that cannot break.

Last Spring

THIS morning at the door
I heard the Spring.
Quickly I set it wide
And, welcoming,
"Come in, sweet Spring," I cried,
"The winter ash, long dried,
Waits but your breath to rise
On phantom wing."

A brown leaf shivered by,
A soulless thing—
My heart in quick dismay
Forgot to sing—
Twisted and grim it lay,
Kin to the ghost-ash gray,

Dead, dead — strange herald this
Of jocund Spring!

I spurned it from the door.
I longed that Spring
Should come with song and glow
And rush of wing,
Not this, not this! — But O
Dead leaf, a year ago
You were the dear first-born
Of Hope and Spring!

Presence

BY a sense of Presence, keenly dear,
I, who thought her distant,
Knew her near.

By an echo that most sweetly woke,
I, long keyed to silence,
Knew she spoke.

By her nearness and the word she said,
I, who thought her living,
Knew her dead.

In an Autumn Garden

TO-NIGHT the air discloses
Souls of a million roses,
And ghosts of hyacinths that died too soon;
From Pan's safe-hidden altar
Dim wraiths of incense falter
In waving spiral, making sweet the moon!

Aroused from fragrant covers,
The vows of vanished lovers
Take voice in whisperings that rise and pass;
Where the crisped leaves are lying
A tremulous, low sighing
Breathes like a startled spirit o'er the grass.

Ah, Love! in some far garden,
In Arcady or Arden,
We two were lovers! Hush—remember not
The years in which I've missed you—
'Twas yesterday I kissed you
Beneath this haunted moon! Have you forgot?

Rose Dolores

THE moan of Rose Dolores, she made her plaint to me,
"My hair is lifted by the wind that sweeps in from the sea;
I taste its salt upon my lips—O jailer, set me free!"

"Content thee, Rose Dolores; content thee, child of care!
There's satin shoon upon thy feet and emeralds in thy hair,
And one there is who hungers for thy step upon the stair."

The moan of Rose Dolores, "O jailer, set me free!
These satin shoon and green-lit gems are terrible to me;
I hear a murmur on the wind, the murmur of the sea!"

"Bethink thee, Rose Dolores, bethink thee, ere too late!
Thou wert a fisher's child, alack, born to a fisher's fate;
Would'st lay thy beauty 'neath the yoke—would'st be a fisher's
mate?"

The moan of Rose Dolores "Kind jailer, let me go!
There's one who is a fisher—ah! my heart beats cold and slow
Lest he should doubt I love him—I! who love not heaven so!"

"Alas, sweet Rose Dolores, why beat against the bars?
Thy fisher lover drifteth where the sea is full of stars;
Why weep for one who weeps no more?—since grief thy beauty
mars!"

The moan of Rose Dolores (she prayed me patiently)
"O jailer, now I know who called from out the calling sea,
I know whose kiss was in the wind—O jailer, set me free!"

A Pilgrim

ACROSS the trodden continent of years
To shrines of long ago,
My heart, a hooded pilgrim, turns with tears —
For could I know
That in the temple of thy constancy
There still may burn a taper lit for me,
'Twould be a star in starless heaven, to show
That Heaven could be.

Bent with the weight of all that I desired
And all that I forswore,
My heart roams, mendicant, forlorn and tired,
From door to door,
Begging of every stern-faced memory
An alms of pity — just to come to thee,
No more thy knight, thy champion no more —
Only thy devotee!

Spring will Come

SPRING will come to help me: she'll be back again,
Back with the soft sun, the sun I knew before.
She will wear her green gown, the emerald gown she wore
When the white-faced windflowers blew along the lane.

Spring will come to help me: When her waking sigh
Drifts across my sore heart all the pain will go.
How shall hearts be aching when larks are flying low,
Low across the fields of camas bluer than the sky?

I've a tryst with Spring here — maybe they'll be few
Now the world grows older — and shall I delay
Just because a Winter has stolen joy away?
What cares Spring for old joys, all her joys are new.

Maybe there'll be singing in my sorrow yet —
I have heard of such things — but, if there be not,
Still there'll be the green pool in the pasture lot,
All a-trail with willow fingers, delicate and wet.

Winter is a passing thing and Spring is always gay;
If she, too, be passing she does not weep to know it.
Time she takes to quicken seed but never time to grow it—
Naught she cares for harvest that lies so far away.

Cosmos

THE tiny thing of painted gauze that flutters in the sun
And sinks upon the breast of night with all its living done;

The unconsidered seed that from the garden blows away,
Blooming its little time to bloom in one short summer day;

The leaf the idle wind shakes down in autumn from the tree,
The grasshopper who for an hour makes gayest minstrelsy—

These—and this restless soul of mine—are one with flaming spheres
And cold, dead moons whose ghostly fires haunt unremembered
years.

The Secret

IF I should tell you what I know
Of where the first primroses grow,
Betray the secrets of the lily,
Bring crocus-gold and daffodilly,
Would you tell me if charm there be
To win a maiden, willy-nilly?

I lie upon the fragrant heath,
Kin to the beating heart beneath;
The nesting plover I discover
Nor stir the scented screen above her,
Yet am I blind—I cannot find
What turns a maiden to her lover!

Through all the mysteries of May,
Initiate, I take my way—
Sure as the blithest lark or linnet
To touch the pulsing soul within it—
Yet with no art to reach Her heart,
Nor skill to teach me how to win it!

I Watch Swift Pictures

I WATCH swift pictures flash and fade
On the closed curtains of my eyes, —
A bit of river green as jade
Under green skies;

A single bird that soars and dips
Remote; a young and secret moon
Stealing to kiss some flower's lips
Too shy for noon;

A pointing tree; a lifted hill,
Sun-misted with a golden ring, —
Were these once mine? And am I still
Remembering?

A path that wanders wistfully
With no beginning there nor here,
Nor special grace that it should be
So sharply dear,

Unless, — what if when every day
Is yesterday, with naught to borrow,
I may slip down this wistful way
Into to-morrow?

Fear

I HEARD a sound of crying in the lane,
A passionless, low crying,
And I said, "It is the tears of the brown rain
On the leaves within the lane!"

I heard a sudden sighing at the door,
A soft, persuasive sighing,
And I said, "The summer breeze has sighed before,
Gustily, outside the door!"

Yet from the place I fled, nor came again,
With my heart beating, beating!

For I knew 'twas not the breeze nor the brown rain
At the door and in the lane!

Resurrection

I BURIED Joy; and early to the tomb
I came to weep — so sorrowful was I
Who had not dreamed that Joy, my Joy, could die.

I turned away, and by my side stood Joy
All glorified — ah, so ashamed was I
Who dared to dream that Joy, my Joy, could die!

The Lost Name

THE voice of my true love is low
And exquisitely kind,
Warm as a flower, cold as snow —
I think it is the Wind.

My true love's face is white as mist
That moons have lingered on,
Yet rosy as a cloud, sun-kissed —
I think it is the Dawn.

The breath of my true love is sweet
As gardens at day's close
When dew and dark together meet —
I think it is a Rose.

My true love's heart is wild and shy
And folded from my sight,
A world, a star, a whispering sigh —
I think it is the Night.

My true love's name is lost to me,
The prey of dusty years,
But in the falling Rain I see
And know her by her tears!

The Happy Traveller

WHO is the monarch of the Road?
I, the happy rover!
Lord of the way which lies before
Up to the hill and over —
Owner of all beneath the blue,
On till the end, and after, too!

I am the monarch of the Road!
Mine are the keys of morning,
I know where evening keeps her store
Of stars for night's adorning,
I know the wind's wild will, and why
The lone thrush hurries down the sky!

I am the monarch of the Road!
My court I hold with singing,
Each bird a gay ambassador,
Each flower a censer, swinging;
And every little roadside thing
A wonder to confound a king.

I am the monarch of the Road!
I ask no leave for living;
I take no less, I seek no more
Than nature's fullest giving —
And ever, westward with the day,
I travel to the far away!

The Dead Bride

WITHIN my circled arm she lay and faintly smiled the long night
through,
And oh, but she was fair to view, fair to view!

Upon the whiteness of her robe the dew distilled, and on her veil
And on her cheek of carvid pearl that gleamed so pale.

(How still the air is in the night, how near and kind the heavens are,
One might a naked hand outstretch and grasp a star!)

I kissed her heavy, folded hair. I kissed her heavy lids full oft;
Beneath the shining of the stars her eyes shone soft.

"Love, Love!" I said, "the day was long"—"Oh, long indeed," she
sighing said.
"I grow so jealous of the sun, since I am dead."

(How sweet the air is in the night, how sweet, sweet, sweet the flowers seem—
But oh, the emptiness of dawn that breaks the dream!)

The Crocus Bed

YELLOW as the noonday sun,
Purple as a day that's done,
White as mist that lingers pale
On the edge of morning's veil,
Delicate as love's first kiss—
Crocuses are just like this.

Ere the robin paints his breast,
Ere the daffodil is drest,
Ere the iris' lovely head
Waves above her perfumed bed
Comes the crocus—and the Spring
Follows after, wing on wing!

Sweet perfection, holding up
Magic dew in topaz cup,
Alabaster, amethyst—
Curling lips which Earth has kissed,
Folded hearts where secrets hide,
Secrets old when Eve was bride!

Beauty's soul was born with wings,
Flight inspires all lovely things—
Would you gather rainbow fire?
See the rose of dawn's desire
Turn to ash beneath the moon?—
Crocuses must leave us soon.

The Vision

"O SISTER, sister, from the casement leaning,
What sees thy trancid eye, what is the meaning
Of the strange rapture that thy features know?"
"I see," she said, "the sunset's crimson glow."

"O sister, sister, from the casement turning,
What saw'st thou there save sunset's sullen burning?
—Thy hand is ice, and fever lights thine eye!"
"I saw," she said, "the twilight drifting by."

"O sister, oft the sun hath set and often
Have we beheld the twilight fold and soften
The edge of day— In this no mystery lies!"
"I saw," she said, "the crescent moon arise."

"O sister, speak! I fear when on me falleth
Thine empty glance which some wild spell enthralleth!
—How chill the air blows through the open door!"
"I saw," she said, "I saw"—and spake no more.

The Miracle

THERE'S not a leaf upon the tree
To show the sap is leaping,
There's not a blade and not an ear
Escaped from winter's keeping—
But there's a something in the air
A something here, a something there,
A restless something everywhere—
A stirring in the sleeping!

A robin's sudden, thrilling note!
And see—the sky is bluer!
The world, so ancient yesterday,
To-day seems strangely newer;
All that was wearisome and stale
Has wrapped itself in rosy veil—
The wraith of winter, grown so pale
That smiling spring peeps through her!

The Homesteader

WIND-SWEPT and fire-swept and swept with bitter rain,
This was the world I came to when I came across the sea—
Sun-drenched and panting, a pregnant, waiting plain
Calling out to humankind, calling out to me!

Leafy lanes and gentle skies and little fields all green,
This was the world I came from when I fared across the sea—
The mansion and the village and the farmhouse in between,
Never any room for more, never room for me!

I've fought the wind and braved it; I cringe to it no more!
I've fought the creeping fire back and cheered to see it die.
I've shut the bitter rain outside and, safe within my door,
Laughed to think I feared a thing not so strong as I!

I mind the long, white road that ran between the hedgerows neat,
In that little, strange old world I left behind me long ago,
I mind the air so full of bells at evening, far and sweet—
All and all for someone else—I had leave to go!

It cost a tear to leave it—but here across the sea
With miles and miles of unused sky, and miles of unturned loam,
And miles of room for someone else, and miles of room for me
I've found a bigger meaning for the little word called "Home."

Wet Weather

IT is the English in me that loves the soft, wet weather—
The cloud upon the mountain, the mist upon the sea,
The sea-gull flying low and near with rain upon each feather,
The scent of deep, green woodlands where the buds are breaking
free.

A world all hot with sunshine, with a hot, white sky above it—
Oh then I feel an alien in a land I'd call my own;
The rain is like a friend's caress, I lean to it and love it,
'Tis like a finger on a nerve that thrills for it alone!

Is it the secret kinship which each new life is given
To link it by an age-long chain to those whose lives are through,

That wheresoever he may go, by fate or fancy driven,
The home-star rises in his heart to keep the compass true?

Ah, 'tis the English in me that loves the soft, gray weather—
The little mists that trail along like bits of wind-flung foam,
The primrose and the violet—all wet and sweet together,
And the sound of water calling, as it used to call at home.

*The Sleeping Beauty

SO has she lain for centuries unguessed,
Her waiting face to waiting heaven turned,
While winds have wooed and ardent suns have burned
And stars have died to sentinel her rest.

Only the snow can reach her as she lies,
Far and serene, and with cold finger-tips
Seal soft the lovely quiet of her lips
And lightly veil the shadows of her eyes.

Man has no part—his little, noisy years
Rise to her silence thin and impotent—
There are no echoes in that vast content,
No doubts, no dreams, no laughter and no tears!

> * A formation of mountain peaks above Vancouver
> Harbor, outlining the profile and form of a slee-
> ping maiden.

Down at the Docks

DOWN at the docks—when the smoke clouds lie,
Wind-ript and red, on an angry sky—
Coal-dumps and derricks and piled-up bales,
Tar and the gear of forgotten sails,
Rusted chains and a broken spar
(Yesterday's breath on the things that are)
A lone, black cat and a snappy cur,
Smell of high-tide and of newcut fir,
Smell of low-tide, fish, weed!—I swear
I love every blessid smell that's there—

For, aeons ago when the sea began,
My soul was the soul of a sailorman.

Down at the docks — where the ships come in,
And the endless trails of the sea begin,
Where the shining wake of a steamer's track
Is barred by the tow of the tugboats black,
Where slim yachts dip to the singing spray
And a gay wind whistles the world away —
Here sad ships lie which will sail no more,
But new ships build on the noisy shore,
And always the breath of the wind and tide
Whispers the lure of the sea outside,
Till now and to-morrow and yesterday
Are linked by the spell of the faraway!

Down at the docks — when the morning's new
And the air is gold and the distance blue,
There's a pull at the heart! But best of all
Is to see the sun shrink, red and small,
While the fog steals in (more surely fleet
Than the smacks that run from her white-shod feet)
And clamours of startled calls arise
From bewildered ships that have lost their eyes;
The fog horn bellows its deep-mouthed shout,
The little lights on the shore blur out
And strange, dim shapes pass wistfully
With a secret tide to a secret sea.

Lake Louise

I THINK that when the Master Jeweler tells
His beads of beauty over, seeking there
One gem to name as most supremely fair,
To you He turns, O lake of hidden wells!

So very lovely are you, Lake Louise,
The stars which crown your lifted peaks at even
Mistake you for a little sea in heaven
And nightly launch their shining argosies.

From shore to dim-lit shore a ripple slips,
The happy sigh of faintly stirring night
Where safe she sleeps upon this virgin height
Captive of dream and smiling with white lips.

Surely a spell, creation-old, was made
For you, O lake of silences, that all
Earth's fretting voices here should muted fall,
As if a finger on their lips were laid!

The Gatekeeper

THE sunlight falls on old Quebec,
A city framed of rose and gold,
An ancient gem more beautiful
In that its beauty waxes old.
O Pearl of Cities! I would set
You higher in our diadem,
And higher yet and higher yet,
That generations still to be
May kindle at your history!

'Twas here that gallant Champlain stood
And gazed upon this mighty stream,
These towering rock-walls, buttressed high —
A gateway to a land of dream;
And all his silent men stood near
While the great fleur-de-lis fell free,
(Too awe-struck they to raise a cheer)
And while the shining folds outspread
The sunset burned a sudden red.

Here paced the haughty Frontenac,
His great heart torn with pride and pain,
His clear eye dimming as it swept
The land he might not see again,
This infant world, this strange New France
Dropped down as by some vagrant wind
Upon the New World's vast expanse,
Threatened yet safe! Through storm and stress
Time's challenge to the wilderness.

Here, when to ease her tangled skein
Fate cut her threads and formed anew
The pattern of the thing she planned
And red war slipped the shuttle through,
Montcalm met Wolfe! The bitter strife
Of flag and flag was ended here—
And every man who gave his life
Gave it that now one flag may wave,
One nation rise upon his grave!

The twilight falls on old Quebec
And in the purple shines a star,
And on her citadel lies peace
More powerful than armies are.
O fair dream city! Ebb and flow
Of race feuds vex no more your walls.
Can they of old see this? and know
That, even as they dreamed, you stand
Gatekeeper of a peace-filled land!

The Bridge Builder

OF old the Winds came romping down,
Oh, wild and free were they!
They bent the prairie grasses low
And made a place to play.

Then, that the gods might hear their voice
On purple days of spring,
They sought the tossing, pine-clad slope
And made a place to sing.

Tired at last of song and play,
They found a canyon deep
And in its echoing silences
They made a place to weep.

Man came, a small and feeble thing,
And looked upon the plain.
"Lo, this is mine," he said, and set
A seal of golden grain.

Upon the mountain slopes he gazed,
Where the great pine trees grow,
Then gashed their mighty sides and laid
Their singing branches low.

He clung upon the canyon's ledge
And from its topmost ridge,
Above its vast and awful deeps,
He built himself a bridge.

A bauble in the light of day,
New gilded by the sun,
It seemed like some great, golden web
By giant spider spun!

The homeless winds came rushing down —
Oh they were wild and free!
And angry for their stolen plain
And for their felled pine tree —

And angry — angry most of all
For that brave bridge of gold!
With deep-mouthed shout they hurtled down
To tear it from its hold —

The girders shrieked, the cables strained
And shuddered at the roar —
Yet, when the winds had passed, the bridge
Held firmly as before!

Still fairy-like and frail it shone
Against the sunset's glow —
But one, the builder of the bridge,
Lay silent, far below!

The Prairie School

THE sweet west wind, the prairie school a break in the yellow wheat,
The prairie trail that wanders by to the place where the four winds
meet —
A trail with never an end at all to the children's eager feet.

The morning scents, the morning sun, a morning sky so blue
The distance melts to meet it till both are lost to view
In a little line of glory where the new day beckons through—

And out of the glow, the children: a whoop and a calling gay,
A clink of lunch-pails swinging as they clash in mimic fray,
A shout and a shouting echo from a world as young as they!

The prairie school! The well-tramped earth, so ugly and so dear,
The piney steps where teacher stands, a saucy gopher near,
A rough-cut pole where the flag flies up to a shrill voiced children's
cheer.

So stands the outpost! Time and change will crowd its widening
door,
Big with the dreams we visioned and the hopes we battled for—
A legacy to those who come from those who come no more.

Calgary Station

DAZZLED by sun and drugged by space they wait,
These homeless peoples, at our prairie gate;
Dumb with the awe of those whom fate has hurled,
Breathless, upon the threshold of a world!

From near-horizoned, little lands they come,
From barren country-side and deathly slum,
From bleakest wastes, from lands of aching drouth,
From grape-hung valleys of the smiling South,
From chains and prisons, ay, from horrid fear,
(Mark you the furtive eye, the listening ear!)
And all amazed and silent, scared and shy—
An alien group beneath an alien sky!

See—on that bench beside the busy door—
There sleeps a Roman born: upon the floor
His wife, dark-haired and handsome, takes her rest,
Their black-eyed baby tugging at her breast.
Her hands lie still. Her brooding glances roam
Above the pushing crowd to her far home,

And slow she smiles to think how fine 'twill be
When they (so rich!) return to Italy.

Yonder, with stolid face and tragic eye,
Sits a lone Russian; as we pass him by
He neither stirs nor looks; his inner gaze
Sees not the future fair, but, troubled, strays
To the dark land he left but can't forget,
Whose bonds, though broken, hold him prisoner yet.

Here is a Pole—a worker; though so slim
His muscle is of steel—no fear for him;
He is the breed which conquers; he is nerved
To fight and fight again. Too long he served,
Man of a subject race! His fierce, blue eye
Roams like a homing eagle o'er the sky,
So limitless, so deep! for such as he
Life has no higher bliss than to be free.

This little Englishman with jaunty air
And tweed cap perched awry on close-trimmed hair—
He, with his faded wife and noisy band,
Has come from Home to seek a promised land—
He feels himself aggrieved, for no one said
That things would be so big and so—outspread!
He thinks of London with a pang of grief;
His wife is sobbing in her handkerchief.
But all his children stare with eager eyes.
This is their land. Already they surmise
Their heritage, their chance to live and grow,
Won for them by their fathers, long ago!

Another generation, and this Scot,
Whose longing for the hills is ne'er forgot,
Shall rear a son whose eye will never be
Dim with a craving for that distant sea,
Those barren rocks, that heather's purple glow—
The ache, the burn that only exiles know!

This Irishman, who, when he sees the Green,
Turns that his shaking lips may not be seen,

He, too, shall bear a son who, blythe and gay,
Sings the old songs but in a cheerier way!
Who has the love, without the anguish sharp,
For Erin dreamingly by her golden harp!

All these and many others, patient, wait
Before our ever-open prairie gate
And, filing through with laughter or with tears,
Take what their hands can glean of fruitful years.
Here some find home who knew not home before;
Here some seek peace and some wage glorious war.
Here some who lived in night see morning dawn
And some drop out and let the rest go on.
And of them all the years take toll; they pass
As shadows flit above the prairie grass.

From every land they come to know but one —
The kindly earth that hides them from the sun —
But, in their places, children live, and they
Turn with glad faces to a common day.
Of every land, they too, but one land claim —
The land that gives them place and hope and name —
Canadians, they, and proud and glad to be
A part of Canada's sure destiny!
What if within their hearts deep memories hide
Of lands their fathers grieved for, till they died?
The bitterness is gone and in its stead
New understanding and new hopes are bred,
With wider vision which may show the world
Its cannon dumb, its battle-flags close furled!
— Dreams? We may dream indeed, with heart elate,
While a new Nation clamors at our gate!

Vale*

LONE Voyager! Thy Ship of Dreams
Spreads its free sail and slips away
Into the distant visioning
That lies behind the end of day.

The restless tide's impatient wave
In from the broad Pacific rolls
And sunset marks a mystic way
To the far-shining Port of Souls.

We, watching on the darkening shore,
Wave you farewell, and strain our eyes
Till that bright speck which is your sail
Is lost in the enfolding skies.

Brave Heart, Sweet Singer! Speed you well
To those dim islands of the blest,
Far — far — and ever farther, till
The end of distance brings you rest!

* For Pauline Johnson (Tekahionwake.)

The Way to Wait

O WHETHER by the lonesome road that lies across the lea
Or whether by the hill that stoops, rock-shadowed, to the sea,
Or by a sail that blows from far, my love returns to me!

No fear is hidden in my heart to make my face less fair,
No tear is hidden in my eye to dim the brightness there —
I wear upon my cheek the rose a happy bride should wear.

For should he come not by the road, and come not by the hill
And come not by the far seaway, yet come he surely will —
Close all the roads of all the world, love's road is open still!

My heart is light with singing (though they pity me my fate
And drop their merry voices as they pass the garden gate)
For love that finds a way to come, can find a way to wait!

The Passer-By

WE are as children in a field at play
Beside a road whose way we do not know,
Save that somewhere it meets the end of day.

Upon the road there is a Passer-By
Who, pausing, beckons one of us—and lo!
Quickly he goes, nor stays to tell us why.

One day I shall look up and see him there
Beckoning me, and with the Passer-By
I, too, shall take the road—I wonder where?

First Love

BY the pulse that beats in my throat
By my heart like a bird
I know who passed through the dusk
Though he spoke no word!

I cannot move in my place,
I am chained and still;
I pray that the moon pause not
By my window-sill.

I have hidden my face in my hair
And my eyes are veiled—
Not even a star must know
How my lips have paled—

Was ever a night so quick
'Neath a moon so round?
I hear the earth as it turns—
And my heart's low sound!

Sad One, Must You Weep

"SAD one, must you weep alway?
Youth's ill wedded with despair;
Ringless hand and robe of grey
Mock the charms which they declare."

Sad and sweetly answered she,
"What are comely robes to me?
I would wear a grass green dress,
Dew pearls for my gems—no less
Now can comfort me."

"Sweet, the shining of your hair
(All forgotten and undone)
Squanders 'neath the veil you wear
Gold whose loss bereaves the sun."

Very sad and low said she,
"What is shining hair to me?
When from out the rain-wet mold
Kingcups borrow of its gold
Sweet and sweet 'twill be."

"Love, O Love! your hand is chill
As a snowflake lost in spring,
Wild it flutters — then lies still
As a bird with prisoned wing!"

Sad and patient answered she,
"As a bird I would be free;
As the spring I would find birth
In the sweet, forgetful earth —
Pray you, let it be!"

Joseph

NEVER in all her sweet and holy youth
Seemed she so beautiful! The tired lines
Etch her white face with look so wholly pure
I tremble — dare I speak to her of aught? —
She is so wrapt in silence. Yet her lips
Part on a word whose honey she doth taste
And fears to lose by uttering too soon.
I know the word; its meaning is plain writ
In the wide eyes she turns upon the Child.
I dare not speak. No word of mine could find
Its way into a soul close sealed with God
And busy with the thousand mysteries
Revealed to every mother. The soft hair
Veiling her placid brow is all unbound,
Ungentle hands are mine but, trained by love,
She might conceive them gentle — yet, I pause —
I'll not disturb her thought . . . . .

What meant those men,
Far-famed and wise, who came to see the Child?
Their gifts lie by forgotten, though the Babe
Smiled on the shining treasure in his hands.
(Those tiny hands like crumpled bits of gauze)
Their sayings were mysterious to me.
"A King!" they said. What King?

The mother smiled
As one who knew; and it is true they knelt
As to a King. The thing disturbs me much!
I'll ask—but no . . . . .

The breathless shepherds, too;
Plain men, blank-eyed with awe, in broken speech
Stumbling some strange, glad tale of midnight sky
A-shine with angel wings! And at their word
Again the mother smiled, as one who sees
No wonder but what well might happen since
A child is born to her. Are mothers so?
And are they prone to dream the careless earth
And distant heaven wait upon their joy?
I'll speak to her . . . . .

What is that in her look
Which answers me—yet leaves me wondering still,
With wonder so like rapture that I seem
Caught up a breathless second into Heaven?
She turns deep eyes upon me, and she smiles,
Always she smiles! Ah, Mary! could I know
The source of that glad smile—what would I know?
I dare not dream, save that the mystery
Is not yet given . . . one day I may know!

A Christmas Child

SHE came to me at Christmas time and made me mother, and it
seemed
There was a Christ indeed and He had given me the joy I'd dreamed.

She nestled to me, and I kept her near and warm, surprised to find
The arms that held my babe so close were opened wider to her kind.

I hid her safe within my heart. "My heart" I said, "is all for you,"
But lo! She left the door ajar and all the world came flocking
through.

She needed me. I learned to know the royal joy that service brings,
She was so helpless that I grew to love all little helpless things.

She trusted me, and I who ne'er had trusted, save in self, grew cold
With panic lest this precious life should know no stronger, surer
hold.

She lay and smiled and in her eyes I watched my narrow world
grow broad,
Within her tiny, crumpled hand I touched the mighty hand of God!

Spring in Nazareth

"THE Spring is come!" a shepherd saith;
Sing, sweet Mary,
"The Spring is come to Nazareth
And swift the Summer hurrieth."
Sing low, the barley and the corn!

Across the field a path is set —
Sing, sweet Mary,
Green shadow in a golden net —
The tears of night have left it wet.
Sing low, the barley and the corn!

The Babe forsakes His mother's knee,
Haste, sweet Mary —
See how He runneth merrily,
One foot upon the path hath He —
Green, green, the barley and the corn!

The mother calls with mother-fear —
Hush, sweet Mary!
Another sound is in His ear,
A sound he cannot choose but hear —
Hush, hush, the barley and the corn!

Far and still far—through years yet dim
List, sweet Mary!
From o'er the waking earth's green rim
Another Springtime calleth Him!
Bend low, the barley and the corn!

Call low, call high, and call again,
Ah, poor Mary!
Know, by thy heart's prophetic pain,
That one day thou shalt call in vain—
Moan, moan, the barley and the corn!

O mother! make thine arms a shield,
Sing, sweet Mary!
While love still holds what love must yield
Hide well the path across the field!—
Sing low, the barley and the corn!

. . . . .

"The Spring is come!" a shepherd saith;
Rest thee, Mary—
The passing years are but a breath
And Spring still comes to Nazareth—
Green, green, the barley and the corn!

Inheritance

THERE lived a man who raised his hand and said,
"I will be great!"
And through a long, long life he bravely knocked
At Fame's closed gate.

A son he left who, like his sire, strove
High place to win;—
Worn out, he died and, dying, left no trace
That he had been.

He also left a son, who, without care
Or planning how,
Bore the fair letters of a deathless fame
Upon his brow.

"Behold a genius, filled with fire divine!"
The people cried;
Not knowing that to make him what he was
Two men had died.

Song of the Sleeper

SLEEPER rest quietly
Deep underground!
Lord of your kingdom
Of murmurous sound.
Hear the grass growing
Sweet for the mowing;
Hear the stars sing
As they travel around—
Grass blade and star dust,
You, I, and all of us,
One with the cause of us,
Deep underground!

Murmur not, sleeper!
Yours is the key
To all things that were and
To all things that be—
While the lark's trilling,
While the grain's filling,
Laugh with the wind
At Life's Riddle-me-ree!
How you were born of it?
Why was the thorn of it?
Where the new morn of it?
Yours is the Key!

Sleep deeper, brother!
Sleep and forget
Red lips that trembled
Eyes that were wet—
Though love be weeping,
Turn to your sleeping,
Life has no giving

That death need regret.
Here at the end of all
Hear the Beginning call,
Life's but death's seneschal —
Sleep and forget!

The Tyrant

ONE comes with foot insistent to my door,
Calling my name;
Nor voice nor footstep have I heard before,
Yet clear the calling sounds and o'er and o'er —
It seems the sunlight burns along the floor
With paler flame!

"'Tis vain to call with morning on the wing,
With noon so near,
With Life a dancer in the masque of Spring
And Youth new wedded with a golden ring —
When falls the night and birds have ceased to sing
My heart may hear!

"'Tis vain to pause. Pass, friend, upon your way!
I may not heed;
Too swift the hours; too sweet, too brief the day:
Only one life, one spring, one perfect May —
I crush each moment, with its sweets to stay
Life's joyous greed!

"Call not again! The wind is roaming by
Across the heath —
The Wind's a tell-tale and will bear your sigh
To dim the smiling gladness of the sky
Or kill the spring's first violets that lie
In purple sheath —

"If you must call, call low! My heart grows still,
Still as my breath,
Still as your smile, O Ancient One! A chill
Strikes through the sun upon the window-sill —

I know you now—I follow where you will,
O tyrant Death!"

The Gifts

I GIVE you Life, O child, a garden fair;
I give you Love, a rose that blossoms there—
I give a day to pluck it and to wear!

I give you Death, O child—a boon more great—
That, when your Rose has withered and 'tis late,
You may pass out and, smiling, close the gate!

The Town Between

A WALL impregnable surrounds
The Town wherein I dwell;
No man may scale it and it has
Two gates that guard it well.

One opened long ago, and I
A vagrant soul, slipped through,
Bewildered and forgetting all
The wider world I knew.

I love the Town, the narrow ways,
The common, yellow sun,
The handclasp and the jesting and
The work that must be done!

I shun the other gate that stands
Beyond the crowded mart—
I need but glance that way to feel
Cold fingers on my heart!

It stands alone and somberly
Within a shaded place,
And every man who turns that way
Has quiet on his face.

And every man must rise and leave
His pleasant homely door

To vanish through this silent gate
And enter in no more —

Yet — once — I saw its opening throw
A brighter light about
And glimpsed strange glory on the brow
Of someone passing out!

I wonder if Outside may be
One fair and great demesne
Where both gates open, careless of
The Town that lies between?

On the Mountain

THE top of the world and an empty morning,
Mist sweeping in from the dim Outside,
The door of day just a little bit open —
The wind's great laugh as he flings it wide!

O wind, here's one who would travel with you
To the far bourne you alone may know —
There would I seek what some one is hiding,
There would I find where my longings go!

To some deep calm would I drift and nestle
Close to the heart of the Great Surprise.
O strong wind, do you laugh to see us?
We are so little and oh, so wise!

The Prophet

HE trod upon the heights; the rarer air
Which common people seek, yet cannot bear,
Fed his high soul and kindled in his eye
The fire of one who cries "I prophesy!"

"Look up!" he said. They looked but could not see.
"Help us!" they cried. He strove, but uselessly —
The very clouds which veiled the heaven they sought
Hid from his eyes the hearts of them he taught!

Give Me a Day

GIVE me a day, beloved, that I may set
A jewel in my heart—I'll brave regret,
If, on the morrow, you shall say "forget"!

One golden day when dawn shall blush to noon
And noon incline to dark, and, oversoon,
My joy lie buried 'neath a rounded moon.

Only a day—it's worth you scarce could tell
From other days; but in my life 'twill dwell
An oasis with palm trees and a well!

Little Brown Bird

O LITTLE brown bird in the rain,
In the sweet rain of spring,
How you carry the youth of the world
In the bend of your wing!
For you the long day is for song
And the night is for sleep—
With never a sunrise too soon
Or a midnight too deep!

For you every pool is the sky,
Breaking clouds chasing through,—
A heaven so instant and near
That you bathe in its blue!—
And yours is the freedom to rise
To some song-haunted star
Or sink on soft wing to the wood
Where your brown nestlings are.

So busy, so strong and so glad,
So care-free and young,
So tingling with life to be lived
And with songs to be sung,
O little brown bird!—with your heart
That's the heart of the Spring—

How you carry the hope of the world
In the bend of your wing!

The Watcher

THE long road and the low shore, a sail against the sky,
The ache in my heart's core, and hope so hard to die—
Ah me, but the day's long—and all the sails go by!

The long road and the dark shore, pools with stars aflame,
The ache in my heart's core, the hope I dare not name—
Ah, me, but the night's long—and every night the same!

Possession

A YOUTH sat down on a wayside stone,
A pack on his back and a staff at his knee.
He whistled a tune which he called his own,
"It's a fine new tune, that tune!" said he.

In his pack he carried a crust of bread,
And he drank from his hands at a brook hard by;
"Spring water is wonderful cool," he said,
"And wonderful soft is the summer sky!"

He looked to the hill which his steps had passed,
He looked to the slope where a brooklet purled,
He looked to the distance blue and vast
And "Ah," cried he, "what a fine, wide world!"

The youth passed on down the winding track
That led to the beckoning distance dim,
And though he carried but staff and pack,
The world and its giving belonged to him.

To Arcady

"TELL me, Singer, of the way
Winding down to Arcady?
Of the world's roads I am weary—
You, with song so brave and cheery,

Happy troubadour must be
On the way to Arcady?"

Pausing on a muted note,
Song forsook the Singer's throat,
"Friend," sighed he, "you come too late,
Once I could the way relate,
Once—but long ago; Ah me,
Far away is Arcady!"

"Tell me, Poet, of the way
Winding down to Arcady?
Haunting is your verse and airy
With the grace and gleam of faery—
Dweller you must surely be
In the land of Arcady?"

Slow the Poet raised his eyes,
Sad were they as winter skies,
"Once, I sojourned there," he said;
Then, no more—but with bent head
Whispered low, "Ask not of me
That lost road to Arcady!"

Tell me, Lover, of the way
Winding down to Arcady?
Some sweet bourne your haste confesses—
Know you paths no other guesses?
Does your gaze, so far away,
See the road to Arcady?

In the Lover's eyes there gleamed
Radiance of all things dreamed—
"Nay, detain me not," he cried
"I am hasting to my bride;
What have roads to do with me,
Love's at home in Arcady!"

The Fields of Even

O STILLER than the fields that lie
Beneath the morning heaven,
And sweeter than day's gardens are
The purple fields of even!

The vapor rises, silver-eyed,
Leaving the dew-wet clover,
With groping, mist-white hands outspread
To greet the sky, her lover.

Ripples the brook, a thread of sound
Close-woven through the quiet,
Blending the jarring tones that day
Would stir to noisy riot.

And all the glory seems so near
A common man may win it—
When every earth-bound lakelet holds
A million stars within it.

A common man, who in the day
Lifts not his eyes above him,
Roaming the fields of even through
May find a God to love him!

I Love My Love

I LOVE my love for she is like a garden in the dawn,
Pale, yet pink-flushed, with softly waking eyes,
And primrose hair that brightens to gold skies,
And petalled lips for dew to linger on.

I love my love for she is like the mirror of the moon,
(A sweet, small moon but newly come to birth)
So full of heaven is she, so close to earth,
So versed in holy spell and magic rune.

I love my love. O words that be too feeble and too few!
I love my love!—as April on the hill

Brings back earth's morning with each daffodil,
So she within my heart makes all things new.

Spring Awoke To-Day

SPRING awoke to-day!
Somewhere—far away—
Spring awoke to-day
From the depth of dream.

Through the air bestirred
Pulse of winging bird,
Through the air bestirred
Laugh of hidden stream.

On the world's cold lips
Fell warm finger-tips;
On the world's cold lips
Woke the glow and gleam!

Spring awoke to-day!
Somewhere—far away—
Spring awoke to-day
From the depth of dream!

In Town

SOMEWHERE there's a willow budding
In a hollow by the river,
Where the autumn leaves lie sodden,
Turning all the pool to brown;
There's a thrush who's building early,
With his feathers all a-shiver,
And the maple sap is rising—
But I'm glad that I'm in town.

Somewhere out there in the country
There's a brook that's overflowing,
And a quaker pussy-willow
Sews grey velvet on her gown;
Rushes whisper to each other

That marsh marigolds are showing,
And those saucy crocus fellows —
But I'm glad that I'm in town.

Long ago, when we were younger,
How those little things enthralled us;
King-birds nesting in the hedges,
Baby field-mice soft as down,
Muskrats in the sun-warmed shallows —
Strange how all these voices called us! —
Hark, was that a robin singing?
When's the next train out of town?

Summer's Passing

A SINGLE branch of flaming red,
A branch of tawny yellow
And every branch in gorgeousness
A rival of its fellow;
Some russet brown and faded green
With golden shadows in between
And mist-hid sun to mellow.

An instinct as of music near —
A breath the wind is bringing,
Broken and sweet, as from a host
Of swift and solemn winging —
A mystery born of light and sound
Wrapping our trancid progress round —
A sighing and a singing!

Thus in a certain lovely pomp
We leave the Summer lying —
These are her funeral banners, this
The pageantry of dying!
The music that we almost hear
Is wafted from her passing bier —
The singing and the sighing!

The Doom of Ys

DO you hear the bell? 'Tis a silver chime
But it ringeth not in the bourne of time.

With the wind it swells, with the wind 'twill sink,
Dying at last by the sea's dim brink.

By mortal hands the bell was hung
By mortal hands 'tis never swung.

When the moon's at full and the long tide creeps
It rings o'er the town that the deep sea keeps —

The town of Ys, that, unafraid,
Cursed God's good bells for the noise they made,

Cursed them well and pulled them down
From every belfry in the town!

For that sin of pride and that pride of sin,
Deathly and soft, a Doom stole in.

It sucked through the stone, it stole through the street,
It rose in the hall, silent and fleet;

Soundless it swept through the market-place
Folding the town in a chill embrace;

No ruth it knew, it heard no call,
Sinner and saint it gathered them all,

Gathered them all, while over them
The bells they had cursed tolled requiem.

Do you hear the bell? When the full moon rides
It rings o'er the town that the deep sea hides!

Time's Garden

YEARS are the seedlings which we careless sow
In Time's bare garden. Dead they seem to be —
Dead years! We sigh and cover them with mould,
But though the vagrant wind blow hot, blow cold,
No hint of life beneath the dust we see;

Then comes the magic hour when we are old,
And lo! they stir and blossom wondrously.

Strange spectral blooms in spectral plots aglow!
Here a great rose and here a ragged tare;
And here pale, scentless blossoms without name,
Robbed to enrich this poppy formed of flame;
Here springs some hearts'ease, scattered unaware;
Here, hawthorn-bloom to show the way Love came;
Here, asphodel, to image Love's despair!

When I am old and master of the spell
To raise these garden ghosts of memory,
My feet will turn aside from common ways,
Where common flowers mark the common days,
To one green plot; and there I know will be
Fairest of all (O perfect beyond praise!)
The year you gave, beloved, your rosemary.

The Coming of Love

HOW shall I know? Shall I hear Love pass
In the wind that sighs through the poplar tree?
Shall I follow his passing over the grass
By the prisoned scents which his footsteps free?

Shall I wake one day to a sky all blue
And meet with Spring in a crowded street?
Shall I open a door and, looking through,
Find, on a sudden, the world more sweet?

How shall I know?—last night I lay
Counting the hours' dreary sum
With naught in my heart save a wild dismay
And a fear that whispered, "Love is come!"

Premonition

LAST night I dreamed
No dream of joy or sorrow,
Yet, when I woke, I wept,

Knowing the brightness of some far to-morrow
Had darkened while I slept!

The Child

I MAY not lift him in my arms. His face I may not see —
Are angel hands more tender than a mother's hands may be?
And does he smile to hear the song an angel stole from me?

The wise King said, "He cannot come but I will go to him!"
O David! did you seek with words to make the grave less grim?
And did you think to cheat, with words, the jealous seraphim?

So! he will learn of heaven — he, who scarcely knew the earth.
All fullness waits the baby eyes that never looked on dearth —
The mystery of death usurps the mystery of birth!

What light has earth to give me for the light that heaven beguiled?
What is the calm of heaven to him who has not known the wild? —
O, we are both bereft, bereft — the mother and the child!

Intrusion

I BUILT myself a pleasant house.
Content was I to dwell in it —
Its door was fast against the wind
With all the gusty swell of it.

It had two windows, high and clear,
With trees and skies to shine through them,
They were acquainted with the moon,
And every star was mine through them.

Its walls were silent walls; its hearth
Held little fires to gladden me —
And though the nights might weep outside
No sob crept through to sadden me.

Then came your hand upon the latch
(Although I had not sent for you)
And all Outside came blowing in
The way I had not meant it to!

Upon the hearth my tended flame
Leapt to a blaze and died in it.
The night sought out a hidden place
I had forgot and sighed in it.

My window that had known the stars
Seemed suddenly not high at all.
The trees drew back; the friendly birds
Swept dumbly by, too shy to call.

Said you: "It is a pleasant house,
But surely somewhat small for two!" —
And at your word my walls fell down,
Leaving no house at all, just you.

The Sea's Withholding

THE ladye's bower faced the sea,
Its casements framed a sea-born day.
She saw the fishers sail away,
And, far and high,
The gulls sweep by
Within the hollow of the sky!

She saw the laggard twilight come
And, chased by rippling wakes of foam,
She saw the fisher fleet come home —
Brown sails a-sheen
Against the green
With shadows creeping in between!

She saw, when it was evening, all
Day's banners stream in crimson rout
Till night's soft finger blurred them out,
And, high and far,
A perfect star
Shone where the keys of heaven are!

"O far and constant star," she said,
"O passing sail, O passing bird,
O passing day — bring you no word

Of winds that steer
His ship a-near?
Where sails my love that sails not here?

"The days in splendid pageant pass,
In lovely peace the nights go by,
And day and night are sweet; but I—
I cannot say
Lo, the bright day!
Can it be dawn and love away?"

Love Unkind

OUT upon the bleak hillside, the bleak hillside, he lay—
Her lips were red, and red the stream that slipped his life away.
Ah, crimson, crimson were her lips, but his were turning gray.

The troubled sky seemed bending low, bending low to hide
The foam-white face so wild upturned from off the bleak hillside—
White as the beaten foam her face, and she was wond'rous eyed.

The soft, south-wind came creeping up, creeping stealthily
To breathe upon his clay-cold face—but all too cold was he,
Too cold for you to warm, south-wind, since cold at heart was she!

Sweet morning peeped above the hill, above the hill to find
The shattered, useless, godlike thing the night had left behind—
Wept the sweet morn her crystal tears that love should prove un-
kind!

Christmas in Heaven

HOW hushed they were in Heaven that night,
How lightly all the angels went,
How dumb the singing spheres beneath
Their many-candled tent!

How silent all the drifting throng
Of earth-freed spirits, strangely torn
By dim and half-remembered pain
And joy but newly born!

The Glory in the Highest flamed
With awful, unremembered ray —
But quiet as the falling dew
Was He who went away.

So swift He went, His passing left
A low, bright door in Heaven ajar —
With God it was a covenant,
To man it seemed a star.

I Whispered to the Bobolink

I WHISPERED to the bobolink:
"Sweet singer of the field,
Teach me a song to reach a heart
In maiden armor steeled."

*"If there be such a song," sang he,
"No bird can tell its mystery."*

I bent above the sweetest rose,
A deeper sweet to stir —
"O Rose," I begged, "what charm will wake
The deep, sweet heart of her?"

*"Alas, poor lover," sighed the rose,
"The charm you seek no flower knows."*

I wandered by the midnight lake
Where heaven lay confessed
"Tell me," I cried, "what draws the stars
To lie upon your breast?"

*The silence woke to soft reply
"When Heaven stoops — demand not why!"*

"Alas, sweet maid, love's potent charm
I cannot beg or buy,
I cannot wrest it from the wind
Or steal it from the sky —"

*Breathless, I caught her whisper low,
"I love you — why, I do not know!"*

You

SLANTING rain and a sky of gray,
Drifting mist and a wind astray,
The leaden end of a leaden day
And you — away!

Light in the west! The sky's pale dome
Gemmed with a star; a scented gloam
Of bursting buds and rain-wet loam
And you — at home!

The Mother

LAST night he lay within my arm,
So small, so warm — a mystery
To which God only held the key —
But mine to keep from fear and harm!

Ah! He was all my own, last night,
With soft, persuasive, baby eyes,
So wondering and yet so wise,
And hands that held my finger tight.

Why was it that he could not stay —
Too rare a gift? Yet who could hold
A treasure with securer hold
Than I, to whom love taught the way?

As with a flood of golden light
The first sun tipped earth's golden rim
So all my world grew bright with him
And with his going fell the night —

O God, is there an angel arm
More strong, more tender than the rest?
Lay Thou my baby on his breast
To keep him safe from fear and harm!

The Vassal

WIND of the North, O far, wild wind
Born of a far, lone sea —
When suns are soft and breezes kind
Why are you kin to me?

Uncounted years above the sea,
Rock-fortressed from its rage,
The fishermen, your fathers, kept
A barren heritage —
Grim as the sea they forced to pay
The sea-toll of their wage.

And lo! The fate which made you hers
And gave you of her best
And set you in a sunny place,
Down-sloping to the West,
Forgot to change your fisher's heart
Serf to the sea's unrest!

Wind of the North! O bitter wind,
I hear the wild seas fret —
In the dim spaces of the mind
They claim me vassal yet!

The Troubadour

THE wind blows salt from off the sea
And sweet from where the land lies green;
I travel down the great highway
That runs so straight and white between —
I watch the sea-wind strain the sheet,
The land-wind toss the yellow wheat!

Song is my mistress, fickle she,
Yet dear beyond all dearth of speech;
Child of the winds of land and sea
She charms me with the charm of each —
Full soft and sweet she sings and then
She sings wild songs for sailor-men!

No staff I carry in my hand,
No pack I carry on my back,
No foot of earth I call my own,
For castle or for cot I lack —
I travel fast, I travel slow,
And where my mistress bids I go!

My gems, the pearl upon the leaf
At mystic hour of the morn;
My gold, the gold that rims the sea
A moment ere the day is born;
And on my breezy couch o' nights
The stars shine down — my taper lights!

Happy am I that sing of love,
Yet from the thrall of love am free;
Happy am I that sing of pain
And quick forget what pain may be!
I sing of death — and lo! To me
Life is supremest ecstacy!

Indian Summer

I HAVE strayed from silent places,
Where the days are dreaming always;
And fair summer lies a-dying,
Roses withered on her breast.
I have stolen all her beauty,
All her softness, all her sweetness;
In her robe of folden sunshine
I am drest.

I will breathe a mist about me
Lest you see my face too clearly,
Lest you follow me too boldly
I will silence every song.
Through the haze and through the silence
You will know that I am passing;
When you break the spell that holds you,
I am gone!

The Unchanged

IF we could salvage Babylon
From times's grim heap of dust and bones;
If we could charm cool waters back
To sing against her thirsty stones;
If, on a day,
We two should stray
Down some long, Babylonian way—
Perhaps the strangest sight of all
Would be the street boys playing ball.

If through Pompeii's agelong night
A yellow sun again might shine,
And little, sea-born breezes lift
The hair of lovers sipping wine,
If, in some fair,
Dim temple there,
We watched Pompeii come to prayer—
Not the strange altar would surprise
But strangeness of familiar eyes!

Ay, should our magic straightly wake
Atlantis from her sea-rocked sleep
And we on some Processional
Look down where dancing maidens leap,
If one flushed maid
Beside us stayed
To tie more firm her loosened braid—
Would not the shaking wonder be
To find her just like you and me?

Indifference

A BIRD, a wild-flower and a tree—
I care for them, not they for me.

I see all heaven in a pool—
But the frog there takes me for a fool.

To this dead thrush a tear I gave—
All Spring shall sing above my grave,

And naught I spend my heart upon
Know lack or loss that I am gone—

A bird, a wild-flower and a tree,
I cherish them; they suffer me!

Last Things

THERE is no one to do it for me,
But I know what I shall do
When the last dawn breaks o'er me
And the last night is through.

I shall set in pleasant order
The little books I knew,
With flowers on the window ledge
In a shallow bowl of blue.

I'll leave the out door swinging,
(As it might swing for you)
And on the clean swept door-sill
Wild roses I shall strew—

So when pale Death comes trailing
Her branch of sodden rue
She'll gather up my gay content
And know contentment too!

Callous Cupid

CUPID does not care for sighs
Does not care for lover's weeping!
Fair One, dry your pretty eyes,
Cupid does not care for sighs,
Laugh with him if you are wise,
Steel the heart he has in keeping;
Cupid does not care for sighs
Does not care for lover's weeping!

The Meeting

SHE flitted by me on the stair—
A moment since I knew not of her.
A look, a smile—she passed! but where
She flitted by me on the stair
Joy cradled exquisite despair;
For who am I that I should love her?
She flitted by me on the stair—
A moment since I knew not of her!

The Piper

I'VE heard the pipes of Pan
Somewhere, just beyond,—
Over the edge of dawn, I think,
Where the clouds hang soft on the world's dim brink,
Where the red suns rise and the blue stars sink,
I heard the pipes of Pan!

Hush! what you heard was the wind,
The feet of the wind through the leaves,
Or the sigh of the waking night as it stirred.
Or a bird's note afar,
Or the deep breath of June,
Or the full of a star,
Or the shimmering skirts of the sea-slipping tide
In the wake of the wandering moon!

Nay! 'twas the pipes of Pan!
Somewhere—just beyond—
My soul awoke with a rapturous sigh
(Would I wake my soul for a night bird's cry?)
I heard the winds of the worlds sweep by
To follow the pipes of Pan!

Stay! 'twas a voice that you heard,
A voice that you love, in the wood,
The vibrating note of a half spoken word—
For the great Pan is slain,
Of his pipings we know not one magical strain,

They have fled down the years of a world that was young
Oh, ages and ages ago!

Nay, 'twas the pipes of Pan!
Somewhere—just beyond—
Far as a star, yet piercing sweet,
A passionate, poignant, rhythmic beat—
Till my mad blood raced with my racing feet
To follow the piper—Pan!

Wanderlust

THE highways and the byways, the kind sky folding all,
And never a care to drag me back and never a voice to call;
Only the call of the long, white road to the far horizon's wall.

The glad seas and the mad seas, the seas on a night in June,
And never a hand to beckon back from the path of the new-lit
moon;
Never a night that lasts too long or a dawn that breaks too soon!

The shrill breeze and the hill breeze, the sea breeze, fierce and bold,
And never a breeze that gives the lie to a tale that a breeze has told;
Always the tale of the strange and new in the countries strange and
old.

The lone trail and the known trail, the trail you must take on trust,
And never a trail without a grave where a wanderer's bones are
thrust—
Never a look or a turning back till the dust shall claim the dust!

Gold

WHEN life wakened in the Spring
All the world was gold and green!
Sunlight lay on everything,
Sailing cloud and soaring wing,
Emerald banks where snow had been,
Drifts of daffodils between.

When Life's pulse beat strong and high
Shone the world in gold and blue!

Canopied with turquoise sky
Summer passed superbly by,
Bluest midnight cupped the dew
Golden morn might sparkle through!

Now that life would rest again
Soft she lies in gold and brown,
Brown the fields and gold the grain,
Brown the little pools of rain,
Gold the leaves that falter down
To brown pavements in the town.

The Materialist

MY soul has left its tent of clay
And seeks from star to star,
'Mid flaming worlds that are to be,
And fruitful worlds that are,
The Voice which spake and said "Live on!"
(When Death said, "You may die")
And sent my spirit wandering
The stairway of the sky.

Still must I seek what on the earth
I sought as fruitlessly—
The world I knew, the heaven I scorned
Lost in infinity:
Alone, and on the ageless breath
Of cosmic whirlwinds spun,
I hurtle through the outer dark
Toward some fantastic sun!—

O God! how happy is the leaf,
A sweet and soulless thing,
Dying to live but in the green
Of yet another Spring—
These heights, these depths, these flaming worlds,
This stairway of the sky
I'd give, had no Voice said "Live on!"
When Death said, "You may die."

Tir Nan Og

THE breeze blows out from the land and it seeks the sea,
O and O! that my sail were set and away —
Fast and free on its wings would my sailing be
To the west: to the Tir Nan Og, where the blessid stay!

The darkness stirs, it awakes, it outspreads its arms,
O and O! and the birds in their nests are still,
The red-browed hill bleats low with the lamb's alarms,
And a sound of singing comes from the slipping rill.

My soul is awake alone, all alone in the earth,
O and O! and around is the lonely night.
As with the sun, would my soul go forth to its birth —
O'er the darkling sea, to the west — to the light, to the light!

Do they say, "Be content with the land of the Innis Fail,
O and O! there is friendship here, there is song."
But they smile to your face, when you turn they stammer and rail
And the song of the singer has tears and is over long!

A call comes out of the west and it calls a name,
O and O! it is soft, it is far, it is low —
Sweet, so sweet that it touches my soul with a flame
That burns the heart from my breast with the wish to go!

       (Translated from the Celtic.)

The Little Man in Green

'TWAS a little man in green,
And he sat upon a stone;
And he sat there all alone,
Whispering.

"One and two," so whispered he.
('Twas an ancient man and hoar)
"One and two," and then no more —
Never, "Three".

Hawthorn trees were quick with May —
"Sir," said I, "Good-day to you"!

But he counted. "One and two"
In strange way.

Fool I was—oh, fool was I
(Who should know the ways of them!)
That I touched his cloak's green hem,
Passing by.

I was fey with spring and mirth—
Speaking him without a thought—
Now is joy a thing forgot
On the earth.

Ere the sweet thorn-buds were through,
Wife and child doom-stricken lay,
Cold as winter, white as spray—
"One and two!"

Now I seek eternally
That grim Counter of the fen,
Praying he may count again—
Counting, "Three".

> * In the bad chance of a meeting with the "Little
> People" the mortal is cautioned not to speak to
> them nor to touch, but to pass by quickly with
> averted eye.—Old tale.

The Enchantress

I FEAR Eileen, the wild Eileen—
The eyes she lifts to mine,
That laugh and laugh and never tell
The half that they divine!

She draws me to her lonely cot
Ayont the Tulloch Hill;
And, laughing, draws me to her door
And, laughing, holds me still.

I bless myself and bless myself,
But in the holy sign,

There seems to be no heart of love,
To still the pain in mine.

The morning, bright above the moor,
Is bright no more for me —
A weary bit of burning pain
Is where my heart should be!

For since the wild, sweet laugh of her
Has drawn me to her snare,
The only sunlight in the world
Is shining from her hair.

Yet well I know, ah, well I know
Why 'tis so sweet and wild —
She slept beneath a faery thorn,
She is a faery child!

And so I leave my mother lone,
No meal to fill the pot,
And follow, follow wild Eileen.
If so I will or not.

I fear to meet her in the glen,
Or seek her by the shore;
I fear to lift her cabin's latch,
But — should she come no more! —

O Eileen Og, O wild Eileen,
My heart is wracked with fear
Lest you should meet your faery kin,
And, laughing, leave me here!

The Banshee

THE Banshee cries on the rising wind
"O-hoho, O hoho-o-o!"
The dead to free and the quick to bind —
(Close fast the shutter and draw the blind!)
"O-hoho, O hoho-o-o!"

Why are you paler my dearest dear?
"O-hoho, O hoho-o-o!"

'Tis but the wind in the elm tree near—
(Acushla, hush! lest the Banshee hear!)
"O-hoho, O hoho-o-o!"

See, how the crackling fire up-springs,
"O-hoho, O hoho-o-o!"
Up and up on its flame-red wings;
Hark, how the cheerful kettle sings!
"O-hoho, O hoho-o-o!"

Core of my heart! How cold your lips!
"O-hoho, O hoho-o-o!"
White as the spray the wild wind whips,
Still as your icy finger tips!
"O-hoho, O hoho-o-o!"

On the rising wind the Banshee cries—
"O-hoho, O hoho-o-o!"
I kiss your hair. I kiss your eyes—
The kettle is dumb; the red flame dies!
"Ochone! Ochone! Ochone!"

The Witch

HER hair was gold and warm it lay
Upon the pallor of her brow;
Her eyes were deep, aye, deep and gray—
And in their depths he drowned his vow.

She wandered where the sands were wet,
Weaving the sea-weed for a crown,
And there at eve a monk she met—
A holy monk in cowl and gown.

She held him with her witch's stare
(A sweet, child-look—it witched him well!)
Upon his lip she froze the prayer,
And in his ear she breathed a spell.

He babbled ever of her name
And of her brow that gleamed like dawn,

And of her lips — a lovely shame
No holy man should think upon.

They hunted her along the sea,
"Witch, Witch!" they cried and hissed their hate —
Her hair unbound fell to her knee
And made a glory where she sate.

Her song she hushed and, wonder-eyed,
She gazed upon their bell and book;
The zealous priests were fain to hide
Lest they be holden by her look.

Most innocent she seemed to be
("The Devil's sly!" the fathers say)
Her eyes were dreaming eyes that see
Things strange and fair and far away.

They stood her in the judgment hall.
"Confess," they cried, "the blasting spell
That holds yon crazid monk in thrall?"
"Good sirs," she said, "he loved me well."

They haled her to a witch's doom,
They matched her shining hair with flame —
But ever through the cloister's gloom
The mad monk babbles of her name!

And, when the red sun droppeth down
And wet sand gleameth ghostily,
Men see her weave a sea-weed crown
Between the twilight and the sea.

Fairy Singing

SHE was my love and the pulse of my heart;
Lovely she was as the flowers that start
Straight to the sun from the earth's tender breast,
Sweet as the wind blowing out of the west —
Elana, Elana, my strong one, my white one,
Soft be the wind blowing over your rest!

She crept to my side
In the cold mist of morning.
"O wirra" she cried,
"'Tis farewell now, mavourneen!
When the crescent moon hung
Like a scythe in the sky,
I heard in the silence
The Little Folks cry.

"'Twas like a low sighing,
A sobbing, a singing;
It came from the west,
Where the low moon was swinging:
'Elana, Elana'
Was all of their crying.
Mavrone! I must go —
To refuse them, I dare not.
Alone I must go;
They have called and they care not —
Naught do they care that they call me apart
From the warmth and the light and the love of your heart.
Hark! How their singing
Comes winging, comes winging,
Through your close arms, beloved,
Straight to my heart!"

White grew her face as the thorn's tender bloom,
White as the mist from the valley of doom!
Swift was her going—her head on my breast
Drooped like a flower that winter has pressed—
Elana, Elana! My strong one, my white one!
Empty the arms that your beauty had blessed.

Killed in Action

MY father lived his three-score years; my son lived twenty-two;
One looked long back on work well done, and one had all to do—
Yet which the better served his world, I know not, nor do you!

Life taught my father all her lore till he grew wise and gray,
She did but whisper to my son before she turned away —
Yet which her deepest secret held only they two might say.

Peace brought my father restful days, with love and fame for wage;
War gave my son an unmarked grave and an unwritten page —
Who shall declare which gift conveyed the greater heritage?

Spring Came In

SPRING came in with a red-wing's feather
And yellow clumps of the wild marshmallow —
O happy bird, can you tell me whether
In distant France they have April weather?
And little pools that are sunny and shallow?

My soul is awake and my pulse is racing —
My heart is aware that the birds are mating —
Oh, my heart's like a cloud that the wind is chasing
O'er the earth's green blur with its silver tracing
To that sad France where there's someone waiting!

O Spring! begone with your too-sweet clover
And all your bees with honey to carry —
Come again when the war is over,
Come, dear Spring, when you bring my lover!
Yet come no more, should he tarry . . . tarry!

From the Trenches

OH, to be in Canada now that Spring is merry,
Happy apple blossoms gay against the smiling green;
Here the lilac's purple plume and here the pink of cherry,
Hillsides just a drift of bloom with clover in between!

Oh, to be in Canada! there's a road that rambles
Through a leafing maple-wood and up a windy hill,
Velvet pussy-willows press soft hands amid the brambles
Fringing round a sky-filled pool where cattle drink their fill.

Oh, to be in Canada! there's a farmhouse hidden
Where the hollow meets the hill and Spring's first footsteps show —

Not a drop of honey there to any bee forbidden,
Not a cherry on a tree but all the robins know!

Oh, to be in Canada, now that Spring is calling
Sweet, so sweet it breaks the heart to let its sweetness through,
Oh, to breast the windy hill while yet the dew is falling —
Waking all the meadow-larks to carol in the blue!

Smile upon us, Canada! None shall fail who love you
While they hold a memory of your fields where flowers are —
High the task to keep unstained the skies that bend above you,
Proud the life that shields you from the flaming wind of war!

The Reasons

THEY sat before a dugout
In the unfamiliar quiet of silenced guns.
And one said:
"Now that it's over
What about a bit of truth?
Let us say why we came to fight —
No frills —
You first, old Fire-eater!" —

One with a whimsical face spoke freely;
"I? — I sought some stir,
Some urge in living,
Some sense in dying.
I sought a mountain top
With a view!"

  "And the answer?"

"I have seen others find
What I sought."

  . . . .

"I don't know that it's anyone's business
Why I came,"
(Another spoke as if unwillingly),
"A girl laughed, I think —
Funny? — Yes, funny as hell!" —

. . . .

His neighbor said,
"I was a business man,
No sentiment,
Nothing of that kind, —
But the band played
And, suddenly, I saw
My country,
A woman, with hands outstretched,
Her back to the wall —"

"U — um," they nodded,
*"She's got a pull,
That old lady."*

. . . .

"As for me," the speaker was abrupt,
"I was afraid!
I saw pictures,
I heard things —
I couldn't sleep
For the Beast that was abroad —
Fear!
That's what brought me!"

. . . .

They sat silent for a moment
In the sun.
Then an older man said briefly,
"We were all afraid . . . . .
. . . But what of hate?
Did no one come because of hate?"

. . . . . .

"Yes — I" —
They looked at this man
Curiously,
But he added nothing,
And no one questioned.

. . . .

A fresh-faced boy spoke modestly;
"Our family are all Army people —
So, of course —
And it's all over now.
We got through.
But it was a near thing —
What?"

To-Day

TO-DAY is a room
With windows upon one side
And upon the other
A door —
Through the windows we may look
But cannot pass;
Through the door we must pass
But cannot look,
And there are no windows
Upon that side.

Memory

A YEAR is a thief
Who comes in the guise of a friend
Saying, "Let us travel together,
We have much to give each other.
See, I hold back nothing —
For what is giving
Between friends?"

Yet when the year departs
He takes his gifts with him —
"Oh, Robber!" we cry,
Aghast and weeping,
"Nay," he replies, "I did but lend.
Still, for your weeping, I will leave you something.

It is not the real thing
But you may keep it always."

Dream

I SEE a spirit
Young and eager,
Beautiful, too, I think,
(Although I cannot see it clearly)
It is, by right of its own being,
One with all lovely, youthful things;
And they, its age-old kindred,
Welcome it
Saying, "Come, you too are one of us!"

. . . .

This spirit is my own happy ghost—
But I, myself,—alas!

Perhaps

THERE was a man, once, and a woman
Whose love was so entire
That an angel, watching them,
Said wistfully, "Would I were no angel
But a mortal,
Loving so, and so beloved!"
. . . . Yet, when these two mated,
A muddied drop, from some forgotten vial of ancestry,
Brought them a child whose mind was dark;
Who lived—and never called them by their names . . .
. . . . They tended her
For twenty years.
Only when she died
Did they weep, whispering,
"Why?"
The years could find no answer,
Though they went questioning
Until the end.

. . . .

Still wondering
They wandered out into the other country . . . .
It was lonely there,
Being parted from familiar things,
And there was no one to answer questions,
But, suddenly,
(As a wind blows or a swallow flies against the sun)
Came a young girl—eager!
She ran to them,
Calling dear names,
(Names that would open heaven)
"Who are you?" they entreated, trembling . . . .
But they knew!—
Had they not dreamed her so
For twenty years?

Glamour

THE knowledge of love
Is like sudden sun upon a river—
The slipping water
Is instantly opaque and glorious.
No longer can we look into it
Counting the pebbles,
Watching the ribboned water-reeds,
Or searching idly
For that something which we lost
(A ring with gems)
It is all glamour, now!
We turn away, shading our eyes.

Friendship

I THOUGHT of friendship
As a golden ring,
Round as the world
Yet fitted to my finger;
I thought of friendship

As a path in spring
Where there are flowers
And the footsteps linger;
I thought of friendship
As a globe of light,
Yellow before the doorway of my life,
A flame diffused
Yet potent against night;
I thought — but thought itself in ruin lies
Since, yesterday, you passed with lowered eyes!

The Returned Man

THEY thought that he would come back
Quieter,
Less boyish,
But still a hero with tales to tell.
So, when there were no tales,
Only blank silences —
When he lay for hours
Staring through leafing branches
And forgot them
Utterly —
They tried to arouse him, saying:
"The war is over."
But when he turned on them
His shadowed eyes
They stammered —
Knowing that they lied!

Epitaph

(For the unknown soldier buried in Westminster
Abbey.)

YOU who died fighting
For me and my little children;
You who are a million
Yet are but one,
I lay upon your grave

A rose and a tear—
The tear is the world's sorrow,
The rose is your joy.

For One Who Went in Spring

SHE did not go, as others do,
With backward look and beckoning;
With no farewell for anything
She passed the open doorway through.

The little things she left behind
Lie where they fell from hands content—
Fame a forgotten incident
And life a season out of mind.

The spring will find her footstep gone,
But spring is kind to vanished things,
Camas and buttercups she brings
With green that tears have brightened on.

And we, who walked with her last year
While April in the lilacs stirred,
Will turn with sudden look or word—
Forgetting that she is not here.